BOODIL MY DOG

PIJA LINDENBAUM

Retold by
Gabrielle Charbonnet

HENRY HOLT AND COMPANY • NEW YORK

This is Boodil, my dog.
She's sleeping in her favorite chair.
My dad used to think it was his chair,
but he knows better now.

Boodil is a bullterrier. She's
the best dog in the whole world.
Her brilliant mind is always
at work. Her guard
is never down.

Bullterriers are very fierce,
strong, and brave.

I bet a burglar would take one
look at her and run for his life.

It's my job to walk Boodil after school. It takes us a long time to get down the steps. My dad says that's because Boodil's a little nutty. But I say it's because she has to make sure there's no trouble waiting for us at the bottom of the stairs. That's the watchdog in her.

Boodil always seems to want to
go in a different direction than
I do. I let her decide, because
sometimes a dog knows best.
It takes longer her way, I have
to admit. But we always end up
at the park, just the same.

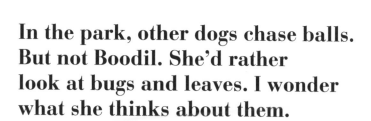

In the park, other dogs chase balls.
But not Boodil. She'd rather
look at bugs and leaves. I wonder
what she thinks about them.

Isn't Boodil beautiful as she sits
on the rock, watching the other
dogs fetch sticks? Nobody decides
when *she's* going to play. She looks
like a royal statue. Her paws
are small and strong, and she
has such pert ears. The fur on
the tip of her nose is very short
and soft. I'm so proud of her.

Sometimes Boodil wanders off
to explore by herself. Last week,
it took me two hours to find her
in the tall grass. Nothing can
stop her when she's on a scent
trail (maybe of a burglar!).

When Boodil waits outside the grocery store,
she likes to watch people and dogs
passing her by. Other dogs seem to want
to play with her, but she isn't interested.
They're not her style.

Little dogs bore her.

But big dogs she loves. Sometimes
I can't figure Boodil out.

We don't like getting caught in
the rain. Boodil is suspicious
of puddles. And she's not fond of
wet paws.

She'd rather avoid them,
if she can.

You'd think Boodil would be glad to get back home where it's dry. But when I call her upstairs to towel her off, something outside usually catches her eye. I yell and yell, but she won't budge. She has nerves of steel.

BOODIL!

Boodil won't eat just anytime—
she eats when she chooses.
I always remind Mom to get
Boodil's favorite foods,
but sometimes she forgets.

Usually, I can get her to eat anyway.

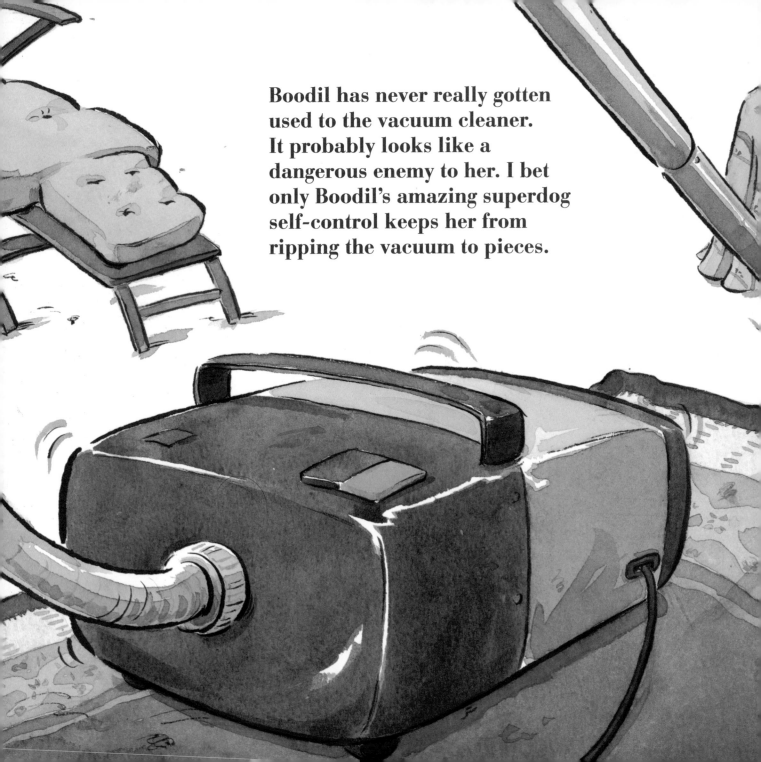

Boodil has never really gotten used to the vacuum cleaner. It probably looks like a dangerous enemy to her. I bet only Boodil's amazing superdog self-control keeps her from ripping the vacuum to pieces.

Every night, I know what's coming.
Nighttime is when Boodil gets frisky.
I always rush through my bath
so I don't miss the action.

She's so cute when she wants
to play. Mom asks why Boodil
can't play outside during the day.
I think maybe Boodil is just
a night person. Some dogs are.

My little brother hasn't learned to get
out of Boodil's way yet. You'd think
he would catch on after a while.
I don't know why Mom gets so
upset. He falls down all the
time anyway.

Like an amazing white cannonball,
Boodil leaps across the room.
What a dog! I'm always impressed when
she clears the coffee table.

Sometimes Boodil performs a happy little dance on the sofa. I yell for Dad to get the video camera, but he ignores me. Then the neighbor downstairs complains about the thumping noises.

Boodil and I are surrounded by party poopers.

UPSY-DAISY, BOODIL!

Finally Boodil has had enough.
We're both ready for bedtime.
Tonight Boodil needs an extra
little push to get up into her chair.

I feel happy when I see Boodil worm her way beneath her blankie. I give her a last pat and tell her good night. I'll sleep soundly tonight, knowing that Boodil is keeping me safe.

Henry Holt and Company, Inc. / *Publishers since 1866*
115 West 18th Street / New York, New York 10011

Henry Holt is a registered
trademark of Henry Holt and Company, Inc.

First published in the United States in 1992 by Henry Holt and Company, Inc.
Published in Canada by Fitzhenry & Whiteside Ltd.,
195 Allstate Parkway, Markham, Ontario L3R 4T8.
Originally published in Sweden in 1991 by
Bonniers Juniorförlag AB, under the title *Boken om Bodil*.

Library of Congress Cataloging-in-Publication Data
Charbonnet, Gabrielle.
    Boodil, my dog/Pija Lindenbaum;
    retold by Gabrielle Charbonnet.
    —1st American ed.
    Adaptation of: Boken om Bodil.
    Summary: Boodil the dog has many endearing qualities
from his bottom-first climb down the stairs to his nightly
"Superdog" exercise routine.
    [1. Dogs—Fiction.]   I. Lindenbaum, Pija.   Boken om Bodil.
II. Title. PZ7.C37355Bo 1992 [E]—dc20   92-13172

ISBN 0-8050-2444-1 (hardcover)
10 9 8 7 6 5 4 3
ISBN 0-8050-3940-6 (paperback)
10 9 8 7 6 5 4 3 2 1

First published in hardcover in 1992 by Henry Holt and Company, Inc.
First Owlet edition, 1995

Printed in the United States of America on acid-free paper. ∞